THE PROPOSITION 5
THE FERRO FAMILY

BY:

H.M. WARD

www.SexyAwesomeBooks.com

COPYRIGHT

H.M. WARD PRESS
First Edition: August 2014
ISBN: 9781630350352

THE PROPOSITION 5

The events in this volume take place prior to The Arrangement 15.

-HM Ward

Chapter 1

Early morning light shines through the heavy drapes lining his walls and forms a thin slit of pure white on the dark carpet. I stare at it, lost in thought. Next to me, Bryan is sleeping. I wrap my arms around him, and his body feels so strong. That's why this is so hard. It makes no sense. Other than the pain, I can't see what's happening to him. It's internal. His body is killing him, second by second. Eventually, he'll take a breath and there won't be another. I can't stand the thought.

My life has been shaped by death. Everyone I care about, everyone except Maggie, is gone. I slip out of the bed, grabbing my phone before heading down the hall. I text her even though I doubt she's up.

I text: *I'm with Bryan. Just checking in to make sure you're okay.*

To my surprise she texts back: *I am, but I have something horrible to tell you.*

Nothing could be worse than losing Bryan. I type back: *Me too. B home in a lil bit n we can talk.*

She replies: *K.*

I tuck my phone into my pocket before picking up Bryan's sweatshirt and tugging it over my head. I pull my hands under the cuffs and wander through the mansion until I find the kitchen. I smell coffee and desperately need a cup. Unfortunately, the beast—Bryan's aunt—is sitting at the table with another woman. They're both dressed in robes. I blink as shock washes over their faces. I can't imagine why she's here so early, not dressed. How weird is that?

Within a heartbeat, Constance is out of her seat and in my face. "How dare you parade around in my sister's home wearing my nephew's things? Get out right now, you little whore!" She tries to slap my face, but I catch her wrist.

Things finally click into place. The way the women were looking at each other, the touch of her hand, the way their eyes linger in that familiar gaze, the fact that she's here when her sister and husband-in-law are gone, and the way Constance turns into a tiger when she sees me—it makes sense. She's been hiding a secret for years, one that could ruin her forever. That's why she puts up with Mr. Ferro's infidelities and why she allows his women to waltz around her home.

Constance is gay—and this woman is her lover. She thought I knew, but I never noticed before now.

She pulls her hand from my grasp and prepares to start yelling again. I interrupt tiredly, "I don't care about your life or your preferences. I understand it's taboo for you to be seen with her. I get that, Constance, I really do. I don't judge you for it, so stop judging me. The only thing of yours that I want is coffee." I shove past her.

Constance's chin is on the floor. Her girlfriend, a woman at least ten years her junior, sits rigid, regarding me fearfully.

Same sex relationships might be cutting edge and trendy in New York, but not among old money families like this one. This would ruin her. It's why she hates me. She thinks I've been walking around waiting to drop a bomb on her life.

When Constance speaks, her tone is skeptical, "You've known for ages and said nothing. Why?"

"Because I don't care about you." I keep my back to her as I pour the dark liquid into a heavy cup. It's too early. Normal people aren't up at five in the morning. They were probably having morning coffee before parting ways for the day. When I turn to speak, both women are staring at me mortified. "I care about Bryan. Have you not noticed anything about him that concerns you?"

Her gaze narrows. "Don't toy with me. I know my family, every single one of them."

"Yeah, well, you might want to talk to him." She locks her jaw, preparing to order me out, but I add, "Time is a funny thing. We all think we have tons of it until it's taken from us—then we realize there was never enough to start with. Use the time you have, Constance. Love the people you love and make sure they know you do. The day may come when you wish you had, but the chance has passed you by."

She stiffens as I speak. "Are you threatening me?"

I laugh out loud at the ridiculousness of her statement. She has no clue. I was referring to me and Bryan, to the constant pool of regret that fills my stomach. We could have been together, but that chance is lost now, time we'll never have.

"You're so wrong about everything, sealed in your little bubble, out of touch with the real world. This isn't your house, so you thought you were safe, but you're never safe, not from time—not from death. Your nephew..." I swallow hard but don't break eye contact. "Make sure his mother finds out. That's all I want."

The assumption I'm making is massive —that Elizabeth Ferro will care whether her son lives or dies. Bryan hasn't told anyone about his illness except me. Jon can see it, but the others have no clue. I don't know how long Bryan has left, but I don't want him to spend it worrying or fighting. I want to be there to protect him and, by alerting the Ferros to his condition, I probably just made that harder to accomplish—but it's the right thing to do. If I had an extra second to spend with my dad... The thought lurks in my mind, sunrise to sunset. When night washes the sky with purple hues of ink and speckles of sparkling amber, I wish I had one more opportunity to say all the things I never had the chance to voice. Now, those thoughts are trapped within my soul, holding me captive. I'll never be free. I never had the chance to say good-bye. I'm giving the Ferros that chance and hoping beyond hope that they don't toss me out on my ass in reward.

Shoving aside my thoughts, I put my empty cup down and walk out, leaving Constance and her lover gaping in my wake. The two women behind me are children playing house. I may be younger than them in years, but my soul feels ancient. It's juvenile to think your life is only about you. Life is about the people around you. How I wish I never grew up, but wishing is time wasted and I refuse to fritter away another second.

Chapter 2

Maggie and I plan via text to meet at a bagel place just after sunrise. The only cars in the parking lot are by the store. The rest of the shopping center is still closed. I haven't been waiting long when she joins me at the end of the line.

"Hey," Maggie says, wrapping me in a hug.

I hug her back, holding her a second too long. She's going to dart again. I know it. She doesn't handle death well. I suppose no one does, but Maggie's seen too much of it. When I release her, I force myself to forgive her in advance. A soul can only take so much abuse before it can't help but react.

It's like Pavlov's dog. The death bell rings and Maggie runs.

I tuck a piece of hair behind my ear and lean against the glass storefront, before shoving my hands in my pockets. "Hey. How've you been?"

The line wraps out the door and down the front of the shopping center with people who've stopped for a bagel and coffee on their way to work. The line inches closer to the food and we move with it, before resuming positions against the glass. My stomach rumbles at the smell of yeast, and I can't wait to taste the soft, warm bread and bite into it, savoring the thick cream cheese. I've learned not to take little things for granted. Bagels help me find my happy place.

I plan to grab one for Bryan too—poppy seeds with butter—just like he ordered in high school. We came here so many times. I stare out at the parking lot, my mind wandering into a memory of Bryan lifting me into a shopping cart and pushing me like a lunatic into the grocery store, laughing the whole time.

Another customer had asked, "What

aisle did you find her on? I want one!"

Bryan just smiled, his eyes sliding over me in the cart. "Sorry, man. This was the only one and she's all mine. I'll never let her go." The memory echoes sharply in my ears. It feels like it could have happened yesterday.

Maggie's voice snaps me back into the present. She shrugs and pulls her purse strap up onto her shoulder. "I'm all right. I think I found us an apartment, but I heard Neil bought you guys a house." She makes a face, well, tries not to make a face, which makes her pained expression even worse. The line moves again and, as we step forward, she blurts out, "Are you really going to marry him? I thought you loved Bryan? Like were totally smitten with the sex kitten. Well, you're the kitten. Guys are what, tigers? Sex tiger sounds wrong." She laughs, but her light laughter fades when she sees my fake smile. "What's wrong, Hallie?"

I try to keep my voice steady, but it quivers without my permission. There's no point in stalling any longer, and besides, I need her. Even though she's going to run, I have to talk to someone while I have the chance. "Maggie, he's dying."

"But, he can't be! He—" Maggie blurts out too many words at once and nearly starts crying. She's the most empathetic person I've ever met. My pain is playing across her face when she stops, squeezes my hand, and pulls me into a bear hug that could pop my head off. "I'm so sorry, Hallie." She wipes away her tears with the back of her hand and looks at my shoulder, not wanting to ask. Every word is like a knife in my side. "What's wrong with him?"

I fill her in with what I know, what's happened so far. My voice goes hard as I come to the end of the story. "We broke up because of his Aunt Constance. She thought I'd ruin her with information I shouldn't have known, so she figured out a way to break us up." Anger I hadn't noticed until now bubbles beneath the surface of my mind. I won't be angry, I can't be. I refuse to waste my time on her or what she did. "Maggie, I couldn't care less about her, but I've wanted Bryan all this time and didn't have him because of her."

"And yet, you don't sound mad. You sound more creepy serene about it." A red brow lifts slightly on her freckled forehead.

I glance over at her as we move with the line inside the little shop, and approach the case of baked bread. Maggie orders first, then I order and pay for our items. Taking our breakfast, we cut back through the line, out the door, and into the parking lot. I stand there in front of her, wanting to speak but unable to find words, then hand over her bagel and orange juice.

My mouth opens twice, but no words come out. I finally look her in the eye and explain. "I'm not mad. Well, I am—but I don't want to be. It's a waste of time and I have no time left. I'm planning on staying with him, Maggie. Whatever time he has left, I want to be there."

"I understand, and I'm here for you." She takes my hand, but I can't look at her.

"Don't make promises you can't keep, Maggie."

"I'm keeping them this time."

"I'd rather know now that you'll vanish. I can handle this on my own. I'm fine, really. I know what this does to you and—" I make excuses for her until she cuts me off.

"No. Last time I wasn't there for you

because Victor was an asshole. I didn't have a choice. It was part of the way he was controlling me, but he's gone now, Hallie. I won't run. I'll be there for you. You won't have to deal with this alone. I promise. We can get through anything, you and me. I won't leave you Hallie. We're sisters. I'll be there this time." She smiles awkwardly and looks at the pavement beneath her boots.

She shifts her weight to her other foot and glances up at me from under too much mascara. Her mouth hangs open for a second and her lip curls, like she doesn't want to say whatever is about to fall out of her mouth. "There's something you need to know, and I don't know if you'll like it or not with everything that's happened, but you need to know. You need to. And I hate to tell you this now, but maybe it's best this way. I'd wait if I thought it would help."

"Maggie, just tell me. What is it?"

She sucks in a bunch of air and spits it out. "Last night while you weren't home, I walked in on what looked like Neil and Cecily doing stuff that was way beyond the friend-zone." Her lips are mashed together as she tries to remain expressionless. I can tell she wants to castrate Neil as she fights to keep those lips of hers in a straight line.

I blink, and that's all. Anger doesn't spew from my mouth and hands don't ball into fists. I don't feel broken or even shocked.

I feel nothing at all.

If I loved Neil, I'd be irate, but I'm not. I nod.

Maggie's worried face pinches together as she pushes her bright hair behind her ear. "I didn't know if I should tell you. I hate him, but I thought you liked the guy." She watches me with such concern that I can't help but smile at her.

My gaze lowers to the ground and I take in a deep breath, before giving her a sideways hug. When I let go, I mutter, "I'm glad you told me. When it rains it pours, huh?" I offer a smile again, but it's fake this time. There are too many memories racing through my mind, and the motion makes my skin feel like it will crack.

"Yeah." She laughs. "At least we don't have to worry about Victor. I owe you big for that. The papers said one of his men killed him in my apartment. If you hadn't dragged me out that night I would have been shot, too."

I'm numb to what I've done—at least right now. Sometimes, when I can't sleep, the thought of what I've done slips into my mind, unwanted. Victor is a nightmare that won't die, but I can't waste my time.

"It's me and you, now," I tell her firmly. She smiles sadly at me and nods. "Maggie, can you go to Neil's place and grab my stuff? There are only a few boxes. I never unpacked, not really. Neil wanted me to, but I shoved most of them into the back of a closet." I pull out my purse and write her a check. "This should cover rent on our new apartment and whatever else we need. Make it pretty, okay? It'll be nice to have a cute new place to go home to when this is over."

Maggie takes the check and looks down at all the zeroes, before glancing up at me. A lock of red hair falls in front of her eyes. "Hallie, I can't take this."

"Yes, you can. Go do it. We need a place to live. I wish I had more to offer, but that fight is for another day. In the meantime, this will put us in a good neighborhood and we'll be comfortable."

"Are you going to sue Neil and Cecily? They pretty much spent all your money."

I nod. "Probably, but not right now. I need to make a phone call." Maggie nods and I dial my bank as we head to my car. I explain to a very helpful bank employee that Neil's name is to be removed from my account immediately and any transactions in progress with his signature are to be transferred to his account. Joint checking was his idea. I rub my hands over my face and sit down hard on the hood of my car. The thing is filthy, but I don't care. The bank employee asks me to come in soon to sign papers making the changes to my account official. When I insist they need to be signed now, she says to come over at my convenience.

I hang up, and stare blankly at the closed doors of the grocery store. "I can't do this again, not so soon." My father's loss still hangs heavy in my heart, threatening to pull me under. My grief hasn't lessened and fame hasn't helped. The only thing that makes me feel better is Bryan and now I'm going to lose him, too.

I can't breathe. Tipping my head back,

eyes full of tears, I look at the sky and the billowy white clouds. The sky was here long before I was born and will be here long after. It makes me feel small, like my life doesn't matter at all.

Maggie bumps me with her boot. "Bagel?"

"I'm not hungry." I was hungry just a moment ago, but now I just don't feel like it.

"Tough shit. I'm taking care of you, which means you eat this or I'll shove it in your face." She's smiling at me. "I'll do it."

I swipe my food out of her hand. "I know you will." Unwrapping the thing, I take a bite and realize that I'm starving.

"Life isn't about death, you know," Maggie says suddenly. She's sitting next to me on the hood, staring at a cloud, picking pieces off of her bagel, and popping them into her mouth one at a time.

"Then what's it about?" I thought I knew at one point, but I have no clue, not anymore. Life seems like a cruel joke.

"It's about the relationships you make, the kindness you offer, and the compassion you show. It's your chance to show the world who you are and what you're made of.

Hallie, you're the strongest person I know. Instead of sitting here crying with me, you should be with Bryan. Here." She hands me the extra bagel. "Check in once in a while and when you need me, I'll come. In the meantime, I'll get our home ready, I promise. Nothing is keeping me away this time. When you need me, I'll be there— whether it's at the hospital, or the funeral home, or just when you need a break."

I pick up a worried vibe from her. "You're not weak, Maggie. We're survivors, me and you." When I say it, I mean to comfort her, but a lump balls in my throat.

She takes my hand and leans in, resting her head on my shoulder. "We'll survive this too—together."

Chapter 3

I don't want to think about Neil, so I head back to the Ferro mansion and sneak inside. It's still early. The only people up and dressed are the servants. They see me and say nothing. It must be strange to live like a statue, day in and day out, with no one but other staff actually acknowledging that you're human. I can't help it. I smile at the butler guy who's always busy, racing off somewhere. He inclines his head in greeting, but doesn't slow.

After he passes, he turns back. "Do you need something, Ms. Raymond?"

I smile and shake my head. "No, it's just nice to see you." I look at him. This man has been a staple in Bryan's life for years. I wonder if he knows Bryan's secret—because nothing escapes him, at least not when we were younger. I remember getting stern looks from him when we were too young and doing things too loudly while Bryan's mom wasn't around. But the guy never ratted us out.

"Likewise, Ms. Raymond. Tell Master Ferro that if he needs assistance, he can ask anything of me." His eyes bore into mine for a moment before he looks away.

He knows.

I nod and go into hyper-girlie drive. Before I can stop myself, I launch my body at him and wrap my arms around the old guy, hugging him in a sloppy bear-style hug. He stiffens with shock and then pats my back. "People will tell you that it will be all right. Over the next few months you'll hear it again and again, but loss doesn't work that way. Things don't go back to normal, but life does go on. Talk to him about it while you have the chance."

My jaw drops. "What? That'd be so mean. I can't—"

"It's not my place, miss, but if you were

my daughter that's what I'd tell you. Dark times are coming, if this man is your ray of light, soak in as much sun as you can, while you can."

I think I understand what he means, so I bob my head up and down slowly. Talking about death with someone who's dying seems mean. We'll end up discussing all the things we wanted to do, but never had the chance. My throat tightens at the thought and my eyes water. "Thank you."

"Any time, Ms. Raymond." He bows his head to me as if I were a queen, and turns to hurry away.

I don't like his suggestion, but part of it calls to me. What if we did talk about it? I shake my head and clench my hands. No! I don't want to! This isn't fair and I can't just accept that I'm going to lose him—not after we finally found each other again. Not after all this time.

By this time I'm on Bryan's side of the mansion, but I stop short of the door. My intention was to tiptoe back to Bryan's room, but I'm caught by the Ferro I fear most—Sean. He's leaning against the wall, his arms folded over his chest. He resembles his mother, every unspoken accusation clearly visible in his eyes. His dark clothes suit him—leather jacket, blue jeans, black shirt, and shitkicker boots. "You and I have something to discuss."

I mean to shove past him. "I have nothing to say to you."

Sean unfolds his arms, and steps in front of me. He's silent and lethal, with crazy vibes radiating off of him like microwaves. Ding! "Well, I have something that you need to hear—about a man named Victor." My breath catches in my throat as my hand presses to my heart. Sean pulls me by the crook of my elbow away from Bryan's door. "Yeah, I thought you knew something about that. The papers are saying one of his men killed him, but the cops are nosing around, asking me questions about a fucking drug lord. I don't like cops and I dislike questions even more. So, tell me, how is it that they tracked you this far? What did you leave behind?"

I laugh, but it comes out way too high. "You think I killed him?" I'm pressing my fingers to my chest, blinking, with my jaw hanging open. Although it's a stellar performance, something gives me away. Sean can see it.

He steps into my space in a threatening way. His voice rumbles, "I know you killed him."

"No you don't," I snap, trying to push past him again, but Sean won't let me move. He blocks the hall with his massive body.

Leaning in close to my face, he whispers softly, "If I know, my mother knows, and you do not want dirty footprints leading straight to her front door. You need to part ways with Bryan and get out of here before they figure it out."

I shake my head and bite my bottom lip. I probably look like a stubborn brat, but I'm not leaving Bryan.

Sean's eyes lock with mine and his voice drops to a lethal whisper. "I can make you disappear."

Something wakes up inside of me, that same protective trait that made me slice Victor's throat in the first place. My spine straightens and I get in his face. "Likewise."

After a thoughtful moment, the man actually laughs. Sean rubs his jaw with his hand. I can't tell if he's amused or thinks

I'm crazy. He finally asks, "Why'd you do it?"

"Why do you think? The man was a murdering rapist. Let's just say he was in the wrong place at the wrong time. Accidents happen and I wasn't going to let anything else happen to my friend. She's the only family I have left." I suck in air, trying to puff up so I'm not so small, but compared to Sean Ferro, I'm a toothpick.

His blue eyes shift to the side before he runs his hands through his hair. "So, you protect your family and let me protect mine. Walk away. Don't pull Bryan into this."

"Into what? Dead people don't pull anyone into anything."

"Victor Campone is alive."

Chapter 4

A tiny squeak escapes my lips and I nearly fall to the floor. My knees give way, but before I go down, Sean grabs my arms. He holds me upright and continues softly. "The cops suspect he's alive. By the time they got there, the body was gone. Due to the amount of blood they found, their natural assumption was that one of his men killed him and dumped the body. The cops were still going down that path until recently when Campone was caught snooping around my hotel. So, unless they saw a ghost, the man is still alive."

"He can't be." I shake my head and my eyes glaze over as I remember that night.

The amount of blood, the way his head hung back and the wound was so deep. "It's not possible."

Sean sighs and looks at me with an expression that's lost somewhere between pity and admiration. Leaning in close, he says, "The cut was too shallow. It's like aiming for the heart and missing. The guy underestimated what you were willing to do once, but he won't underestimate you again. And I'd bet anything that he'll remain dead for a while, letting others do his dirty work, until it suits him to stage a resurrection."

"How do you know all this?"

He swallows hard, his gaze shifting away and then back to my eyes. "Periodically, our business ventures overlap. I hear things. And I can tell you that if I hear it, my mother has heard it and you sure as hell don't want to piss her off. If Campone ends up here, you're dead. If he doesn't kill you, my mother will."

He grabs my shoulders and urges me, "Hallie, take your friend and get the hell out of here before Campone finds you." Sean releases me. "This was a courtesy warning. If you stick around and Bryan is killed because of you, well, you better hope Victor finds you before I do." His eyes flick over me once, his intentions clear.

I stand there for a second barely breathing. Our eyes are locked, we're both defiant to the core, but he doesn't know— Sean doesn't know about his cousin. Maybe I should take Bryan and run, but I can't. Not while he's sick. He'll need help and hospice care. I can't give him those things if I run. My voice cracks when I speak. "I can't."

"It's not optional."

"No, you don't understand. I can't leave. I can't outrun Victor, and I won't. I'll take care of this. I'll finish what I started." I have no idea how, but I will. If I don't, he'll come after me and Maggie. The man is ruthless, he'll never stop hunting us. I know that for certain.

Sean's dark brow lifts. "Are you insane? You'll never get another chance to kill him. He thought you were insignificant before, now he knows better."

I shove past him. "I'll take care of it. He won't come here, and this time when I kill him, he'll die."

"Hallie," Sean almost pleads my name—almost—but I don't stop.

I head into Bryan's room and close the door. I stay there for a second and tip my head back, breathing hard. I've never even punched a person before this. Now I just confessed to the scariest Ferro of them all that I'm going to take out the city's most notorious drug lord. Super fuck.

I'm still holding the bag with Bryan's breakfast. When I tighten my fist, the paper makes a crackling noise and he sits up. A beautiful smile brightens his ashen face. "Hey, Beautiful Girl. Where'd you run off to?"

"To grab some breakfast and get some dirt on your aunt. It's been an interesting morning." I smile worriedly at him and hand over the bag.

"Dirt on my aunt?"

I shake my head and sit down next to him on the bed. "Yeah, I figured out why she hates me. She thought I knew something all these years, but I didn't figure out what I knew until this morning."

Bryan unwraps his bagel while I'm speaking and bites into it. His green gaze flicks up to mine. With his mouth full, he prompts me. "Well?"

I think about keeping her secret, but I feel no loyalty to her. Besides, Bryan won't tell anyone. "She's gay. I caught her with her lover in your mom's kitchen this morning."

His jaw drops and the piece of bagel falls out of his mouth and onto the bedspread. "No way."

I nod and look down at the piece of food. "Shocked much?"

"Hell, yeah. She's so demure and proper." His nose scrunches at the thought of his aunt being sexually anything.

"And apparently she likes girls."

Bryan blinks and smiles. "Well, that explains a lot of things."

"Yeah, like why she's still married and allows half-dressed whores to walk around her house."

Bryan grins. "Of course, everyone likes a little eye candy."

I bump his shoulder. "Bryan!"

"Come on, think about it. There's been a mistress in that house since Jon was a baby. It's the weirdest family I've ever seen. My mother wouldn't have tolerated it. I've always wondered why Aunt Constance did."

"Your dad doesn't have a live-in whore?"

He tilts his head at me. "My dad doesn't have time for it. He's too busy making money to be bothered with relationships or buying ladies. But still, Aunt Connie likes the ladies. Who would have thought?" He shakes his head. "Then what the hell did I see the day we broke up?"

Good question. I sigh and have a pretty good idea of who to ask. I grin wolfishly. "Which room does Constance use when she's here?"

Bryan looks confused and then his eyes widen. "Are you insane?"

"Only a little." I laugh and almost pinch my fingers together.

Chapter 5

A few minutes later, I'm knocking on the door to the guest room. A snippy voice shouts, "How many times have I told you to —" when Constance's lover opens the door, she looks shocked. "Oh, it's you."

Bryan is standing next to me. "Is this the same woman you saw when we were together?"

"Yeah, I'm pretty sure it's her. I didn't know they were a couple at the time."

Constance, magically appears from behind and shoves us into the room, snapping, "How dare you waltz in here and act like this!" She's livid. I can practically see the steam coming out of her ears. She gives her lover a look and the other woman disappears into another room within the suite.

"Aunt Connie," Bryan begins, but she cuts him off.

"Constance, Bryan. For God's sake, use the right name." She pinches her brow and sits down hard on an absolutely beautiful round tuffet.

"Aunt Constance, I wouldn't have looked down on you for this. Why didn't you tell anyone? And why the hell did you break us up? Hallie didn't even know."

Constance's eyes flick up and her gaze widens. "Of course she knew. She saw me with my arms around another woman. How could she not know?"

"I didn't know. I assumed you were affectionate with your friends. I was interested in Bryan, not you."

Bryan blinks slowly and I can tell he's in pain. "Just tell me what I saw."

Constance smiles and folds her hands on her lap like she's posing for a picture. Socialite in a robe. It's very dramatic and she looks like all she wants is world peace. She's more fake than a plastic plant. "I don't know what you mean."

"Cut the crap, Aunt Connie. I saw a girl at the park years ago. Jon said that she was Hallie, but I never saw her face because she was making out with someone. We broke up because Hallie cheated on me, but Hallie never cheated on me and has no idea what I'm talking about. Some other people seem to know about it, though, and I'm guessing you have every last detail."

She sits there, confident. "I'm afraid not."

"Then, I'm afraid I might forget about your little secret here and let it slip next time I see Mom and Dad." Bryan takes my hand and we turn to leave, but Constance jumps up, blocking the door.

"Don't you dare!"

"Then, tell me!" Bryan yells. "Tell me what you did! I deserve that. You stole my happiness by taking away the only woman I ever loved. I'm lucky to have her now. I need her, and you cost me years." He says the last word like it pains him. Bryan grabs a dresser and inhales slowly, deeply. His face pinches together and, though it appears to be anger, I know it is pain. "Tell me."

Constance sighs dramatically and throws up her hands. "Fine. It was your sister with some boy Jon knew. They set it up. Joselyn went to that dumpy Mandee's store and bought a dress that resembled Hallie's favorite. We'd seen her in it several times. Then Jon called you."

Bryan shakes his head. "But her hair?"

"Wig." She shrugs like it was no big deal. "The hair stylist was amazing. Jos looked like a replica from a distance. If you got too close, you would have noticed, but you didn't so it all worked out."

Bryan laughs bitterly and steps toward his aunt. "I haven't told anyone this yet, but I want you to be the first to know. I'm dying, Aunt Connie. There's not a fucking thing they can do to help me, and you took the only woman I've ever loved away from me to hide your own selfish secret. I don't care who you fuck, and neither did Hallie. I never want to speak to you again. I never want to see your face again. I only have a handful of days left and I'm not wasting a single second more with you. Goodbye Aunt Connie." He turns and holds out his elbow for me. It looks gallant, but that's not why he does it. It's because his strength has been sucked from his body. The confrontation stole it, funneling it away from him swiftly.

For once his aunt is silent. The door closes behind us and Bryan doesn't look back.

Chapter 6

When Bryan returns to his room, he downs a few pills and does a couple of shots. His stomach is empty so it hits him hard. I take off my clothes and press my body to his. I want to hold him for a while. As he wraps his arms around me, pulling me close to his body, I can tell that he's dropped a few pounds this week. Just after Bryan settles back into the bed, Sean bursts in.

Bryan is wearing a pair of jeans and only jeans. I'm not wearing anything, so I pull the sheet up, ready to beat Sean to a pulp if he picks a fight now. "You." he says, lifting his hand and pointing a finger at Bryan.

Bryan just laughs and ignores him. "Get out, you crazy fucker."

Sean works his jaw while folding his arms over his chest. "How do you know Victor Campone?"

Bryan's smile fades. "What's it to you? Besides, he's dead." He glances at me and I give Sean a look that says shut up, but he doesn't.

"What the fuck is this? It's not even nine in the morning and you're already high? Who gave you this shit?" Sean is holding a bottle of pills.

Bryan gets up to fight, but I jump in front of him, clutching the sheet around me. "They're mine. Give them back."

Sean glares at me. "Yeah, why are you popping these? Life too hard, Princess?"

"Fuck off, Sean." Bryan has a warning tone that says to drop it and get out.

"You two are going to end up dead! You're the dumbest couple of assholes I've ever met." Sean takes the bottle and starts to dump them down the drain. I scream no, and launch myself at him knocking the other half of the bottle onto the floor. White pills go flying everywhere.

"You don't know everything!" I scream in his face. "So back off! Those weren't from Victor. I'm not stupid and neither is Bryan." I glare at Sean. Bryan doesn't know about Victor and this idiot is spelling out the kind of trouble I'm in. Take a hint and shut the hell up!

Bryan's gaze is burning holes into Sean's chest. "Get out." His voice is low and deadly.

Sean hisses, "Bryan, I swear to God, if you pull Jon down with you—"

"He won't." Constance's voice is calm and even. She's standing in the threshold and pushes her way into the room. She glances at her nephew and tells her son, "Come along. We have things to discuss."

Sean's wide sapphire eyes flick from me to Constance and back. "What the fuck?"

Constance seems somber. She snaps her fingers and points to the floor next to her. "Come, now. It's not an option."

Sean, irritated beyond words, growls, shoves past his mother and is gone without another word. That's when she looks over at Bryan. "A team of specialists will come by later today. They've been paid to keep their silence."

"It's unnecessary." Bryan replies and sits down hard on the edge of his bed.

"Perhaps, but let them look, just in case something was missed. Don't give up hope until you breathe your last breath. Do you understand?" She looks down at him, and has her typical matriarch demeanor, but it's stern, yet soft. When Bryan doesn't answer she adds, "Cancer runs rampant in our family. This team of doctors are the best in the world. If you don't want to humor me, at least let them look you over for Hallie."

Bryan straightens and glares at her, "Don't you dare."

Constance smiles and it looks perfectly malicious. "I would never try to take you away from her. I owe you something for my error all those years ago. She can stay."

"Write it."

"What?" Constance blinks, looking stunned.

"Write it down and sign it. I want the notary here as well. After that's done, you can tell whoever you want."

"Just let the doctors look you over. Then this silly need for signatures and a notary aren't needed."

Bryan lifts a brow at her. "Do it. There's something else you'll want to know and I'm not saying a damn thing until the notary is here."

Constance seems annoyed and then her gaze flicks to mine. "I keep my promises."

"I wouldn't know." I reply coldly.

Bryan looks at Sean who stands behind his mother. He's pieced everything together, I can see it on his face. Sean interrupts. "I'll do it. Who else do you want here?"

"Jon and Jos."

Sean nods once. "Done." He leaves the room quickly, and although he didn't react, I know the realization that his cousin will soon be gone struck him hard. It's the way his shoulders stiffened and his jaw locked. The movements were minor, but I saw them all the same.

Chapter 7

"You can't be serious?" Jos blinks and folds her slender arms over her chest. "You can't do this. We'll contest it. You know we will."

Jon glances at Sean, but says nothing. Bryan is sitting up in bed and I'm next to him wearing a pair of his sweats.

His arm is around me, possessively, protectively. "I know, which is why I had this drawn up. Sign it." Bryan has been holding an envelope. He lifts it, handing it to Jon. His cousin opens the letter and picks up a pen, scratching his name across the bottom before passing it to his mother.

Constance's eyes flick over the letter and

she shakes her head. "No, this is not how these things work. You can't hand over your part of the estate to a stranger. Even if you married her, and you died, she still wouldn't be given this amount of money. You've lost your senses, Bryan. I cannot sign this. I cannot promise you that I won't contest this decision."

Jon speaks firmly. "She's not a stranger and she would have been his wife if we hadn't meddled."

His mother gives him a look that could kill a bear. "No, I'm not signing this. You've been ill for some time and your mental facilities have been compromised. No judge in his right mind would allow this will to stand. This is Ferro money, not hers."

Sean has been standing next to Joselyn. He's leaning against the wall, silent. Bryan's sister keeps switching between denial and rapid blinking, as if she's trying not to cry. "He's not that sick. I've seen him every day. He's been laughing!" As if that explained everything. She covers her mouth with her hand and rushes out of the room.

Bryan sighs loudly and nods at Sean. "Go get her."

Sean rushes after Jos, closing the door behind him.

I had no idea what Bryan wanted, but now that I'm looking at it, I'm afraid to speak. He wants me to be his heir. Some of his things are part of the Ferro estate and this amount of money is more than I got for book sale and movie rights combined. I want to tell him I can't take this, but he sees it in my eyes. Bryan strokes my cheek and says softly, "I want to take care of you, even after I'm gone. Hallie, let me. Please."

"I love you, and you don't have to prove a thing to me. Besides, I have enough money, even with Neil buying the house and spending most of my advance." Ooops. I hadn't told him that part, yet.

Bryan looks furious. He's ready to jump out of bed. "That fucking son of a—"

Pulling his arm, I plead with him. "Stop! Bryan, you can't fix everything and I don't want you to. Time with you is so much more precious than trying to get that money back. Plus I have a huge ass house. I know I can take it from him if we went to court."

Constance rolls her eyes. "Naivety is unbecoming, dear. How did you allow him to spend your entire fortune? Getting courts involved will create a public scandal, not to mention that it's a waste of time and money." She looks at Bryan, as if I proved her point. "See, Bryan? This is why you shouldn't do it. New money always makes mistakes like this, and I won't see the Ferro fortune frittered away with such irresponsibility. My final answer is no and no judge will uphold this will." She turns on her heel to leave.

But Bryan pushes off the bed and pads across the room with that smile he always wears, the one that hides his pain. "Aunt Connie, you obviously didn't read it."

She stops and turns, looking him over like she can't believe he's so ill. "There's no point. It won't stand."

His grin broadens as he asks Jon for the papers. Handing the will out to his aunt, Bryan says simply, "Read the date."

She glances at him and then down at the papers that were shoved into her hands. Something changes in that second and his aunt stiffens. She stares at the will in disbelief as her lips mash into a thin line. When she glances up at Bryan, there's fire burning in her eyes. "You went behind my back and did this, even after what you saw?"

Bryan's false smile vanishes. His voice drops to a deadly whisper. "After I saw my sister making out with some guy Jon knew? Is that what we're talking about?" Jon goes white. It's like someone flipped a switch. His jaw drops as his eyes go wide. He tries to interrupt, to say something to his mother, but Bryan doesn't let him. "I'll deal with you later," Bryan snaps at Jon before returning his gaze to Constance.

"You can contest it all you want, but I have a strong feeling you won't. If the rest of the family supports me, the court will too, and then you'll have the scandal for nothing. Imagine what the papers would say when they find out the erotic man in Hallie's book is a Ferro. Imagine what that would do to the family, Aunt Connie. Imagine your name added to the trash that gets printed when they find out about your little secret."

Constance's eyes narrow to slits as she steps toward her nephew. "She wouldn't dare."

Bryan laughs once. "No, she wouldn't, but I would. I'll have reach beyond my grave, I promise you that. If you harm her, your little secret will spread faster than crabs in a whore house."

Constance scrunches up her nose in disgust. "You defied me."

"You can't control me anymore. No one can." Bryan blinks rapidly and sucks in air. His eyes press closed and he grabs for the dresser by the wall, but he's too far away.

Jon lunges for him, grabbing his cousin by the shoulder—under his arm—to keep Bryan from crashing to the floor, while his mother does nothing to help. "Come on, Bryan."

Jon tries to pull Bryan away, but he doesn't budge. Instead, he shakes off the help and looks his aunt in the eye. "I know what you're thinking and you're wrong. Again. Trust me for once, call it a parting gift."

Constance looks at the will, her angry eyes studying the papers. "She can have whatever is in your accounts and the things you've given her, but nothing—not a cent— is coming out of your inheritance."

"Fine. Sign it."

"But you don't have this kind of money,

so where is it coming from?" As she speaks, Sean slips back into the room with a tear-streaked Jos in tow.

Bryan is weak and irritated. I know his head is throbbing and from the way he's blinking, I doubt he can see any longer. Handing me his phone, he tells me to open an app. "Go to the banking app and show it to everyone."

I do as he asks, and my jaw drops when his accounts open. "Holy shit!"

My outburst shocks Joselyn into action. She rushes over to look at the screen on his phone, then stares at her brother as if she doesn't know him. "Where did you get that?"

Jon takes the phone and blinks once, trying to hold back a smile before passing it to Sean. His brother looks at it once, impressed, and then hands it to his mother. Constance inhales slowly, puffing up. "Answer her. Is this drug money?"

"Are you fucking serious? No, it's not drug money. I've been high for the past few months because of prescription pain meds, not illegal drugs. What the fuck is wrong with you people? Can't a guy earn an honest living?"

Jos speaks first. "Yes, but you don't work."

Bryan sighs and settles back into the pillow. "I did and I do. I'm a day trader. Flick the screen, it'll pull up the recent trades." His twin does as he asks and her eyes get bigger. "I take large sums of money and put them into high risk stocks. When it pans out, I get a small fortune every time."

"But when it doesn't, you lose a small fortune." Jos looks at her brother, while Jon studies the numbers from over her shoulder.

I say softly, "I didn't know you did that."

He smiles at me. "I didn't tell anyone. It's risky and not exactly an orthodox way of earning a living as far as my family is concerned. I'd rather work smarter, than harder. Plus, this is the only way I could work some days, especially lately."

A shocked silence settles over the room. Not only is Bryan charming and rich by birth, but he's more than tripled his fortune and no one knew about it. To them, it looked like the man sitting next to me did nothing but play and have fun.

Bryan pulls me to him until my head

rests against his chest. He holds on tight and stares them down. "Sign the will. It's clearly my money and there is no doubt as to my mental state when this was drafted."

I look up at him. "When did you decide to leave everything to me?" I know it had to be before the illness.

"The day we broke up. I wanted this money to come at you like a brick to the head. I wanted to ruin whatever happiness you had, to force you to tell your husband who I was and what we did. My intentions weren't noble, Hallie, so don't act like they were. I wanted to hurt you as much as you hurt me. I never dreamed I'd been led astray by my best friend," he gives Jon a harsh glance. "Then when I found out I was sick, I didn't change it. I had planned on staying away from you, but when you popped up on TV with that book—I couldn't stay away."

"I'm glad you didn't."

"So, you're not mad?"

I laugh and hug him hard. When I let go, I look into his eyes. "Losing you was my biggest regret. I'm glad you didn't stay away. All I want is you, Bryan. You can do anything you want with this money. I don't need it."

"Maybe not, but I need for you to take it. I need to have peace of mind when I breathe my last breath, knowing that no matter what trouble comes your way, you have means to escape. Plus it's a present, so you can't return it." He smiles at me, and kisses my cheek.

I feel so awkward. His family is so upset, but there's no swaying Bryan. I don't want him fighting with everyone as he slips away. I don't want him to pass in anger, I try to tell him no again, but before I can speak, his sister takes the will from her aunt and signs it.

"I won't contest it. It's yours." She lets out a shaky breath and adds, "I'm so sorry. Both of you need to know. I had no idea how much she loved you. It didn't look that way to us. I shouldn't have done it. God Bryan, I understand if you can't forgive me. I can't forgive myself." Her voice is shaking and her eyes are glassy. Tears will fall in a moment. Jos turns to me. "Hallie, you're welcome here. I'll make sure of it, for as long as you want. I'm so sorry." She chokes up and the last word doesn't come all the way out, before she turns and races out of the room again. We hear her sobs as she retreats down the hall.

Sean takes the papers from his mother and signs them. "And I thought you were a slacker." Sean shakes his head, smiling as he leaves the room.

Jon clears his throat, but Bryan doesn't look at him. "I can't make up for what I did."

"No you can't." Bryan replies bitterly.

"It wasn't meant to hurt you. I swear to God, Bryan. I thought she was after your money."

"We think that of everyone, Jon. I could have easily said the same thing about Cassie way back when. Even now. Money would give her a freedom she doesn't have. That said, would you rather I kept it from you?"

"I don't follow." Jon shakes his head and steps closer.

"You thought something bad about the woman I loved and didn't bother to tell me your suspicions. Instead, you acted on them without consulting me first. It should have been my choice, my decision—not yours. What even made you think she didn't care about me?"

Jon looks like he ate a goat and its horns are stuck in his throat. "Bryan, I don't think it's worth repeating, not now."

"I do. Tell me."

Jon looks at me, but I have no idea what he's going to say. "I saw her books. They were covered with your name and 'Mrs. Hallie Ferro.' That concerned me, but then I overheard her talking to someone, saying that she was dating some rich guy who would give her money whenever she asked."

My brow crumples. "I never said that."

"She never asks for money, and never has." Bryan stares at Jon, perplexed.

"I saw her walk into the locker room and heard her voice. I thought it was her, but I must have been wrong. I wouldn't have done it on a whim, Bryan. I was certain. And now the only thing I can say is that I'm sorry."

Suddenly, I feel sick inside. I know what he's talking about. Maggie and I used to joke about marrying rich men and making them buy us all sorts of expensive things. Jaw trembling, I say, "I did say that." Everyone looks at me. "It wasn't about Bryan, though.

One of the ways Maggie and I dealt with our pasts was to dream about a future where we had gorgeous husbands with tons of money to take care of us. We'd joke about buying yachts and mansions. She'd add a new wing to her mansion and I'd add another jet to my private fleet. It was a joke. Maggie didn't even know we were dating. The book you saw was my journal, and I have no idea how you saw it since it was in my locker and not out in the open."

Jon smiles awkwardly. "I'd rather not say."

I turn and glance at Bryan. "I never wanted your money. I just wanted you."

He kisses my forehead and pulls me closer. "I know, baby. I know." After a moment, he holds a hand out to Jon. "I have her now. Promise me you'll watch out for her when I'm gone."

Jon swallows hard and nods before taking his cousin's hand. Jon shakes and then says, "Fuck it." He leans into us and embraces us both, smashing us together in a bear hug. When Jon straightens, he rushes out of the room without another word.

That leaves his aunt standing there, the

will clutched in her hands. We watch her for a moment. Her back is rigid in her perfectly pressed outfit. When she speaks it sounds like she's going to sign. "Bryan, I can't imagine what you're going through—what you've been through. I know I'm responsible for some of the pain that's bestowed you and for that I apologize, but one misstep does not correct another. I cannot allow this. I'm sorry." She drops the paper on the bed and walks to the door. Before leaving, she says over her shoulder. "Hallie, make sure he allows the doctors to look him over. Now isn't the time to argue."

"Now is the only time you have." I press my lips together and look after her, mentally pleading with her not to fight with him, not now. The time for fighting is over.

Constance's cold eyes meet mine, but she doesn't answer. Instead the older woman pushes through the door and doesn't look back.

Chapter 8

Bryan doesn't want the doctors to look him over, so I invite them to camp out in his room until he reluctantly gives permission. I know he doesn't want to get his hopes up, and doing this is enough to mess with his head horribly. The slightest glimmer of false hope will crush him.

The medical team is wearing street clothes, no scrubs or lab coats on any of the four doctors. The first man is young, maybe thirty with a goatee and a shaved head. There's an older woman, an oncologist, with a clipboard. While the others speak, asking questions and conferring with one another, she scribbles constantly, saying nothing.

When she first arrived, I thought she was their secretary. She nearly bit my head off for that mistake, but in regard to her work, the woman doesn't talk. She just circles Bryan and jots things down. The third doctor is older, with frizzy white hair sticking off his skull and a quirky plaid shirt and stripe pants clothing combination. He looks like he escaped from the loony bin. They've been looking at him for an hour now, but it feels longer. Why does time seem to crawl by when things matter most? Under their inspection, my love is acting like a hurt little boy. I want to wrap my arms around him and throw them out, but this is his last chance, our last chance.

"But if there's something they can do—"

Bryan's jaw is locked. He's sitting on the edge of his bed, shirt off, and glares at me. "No one knows what I went through to get this diagnosis in the first place. Sitting here, repeating the process is unnecessary and cruel. I thought you'd understand that."

"Different eyes might see different things."

"Different eyes won't miss the massive

tumor in my head, Hallie." His words are so pointed that my gaze drop to the floor. He softens. "I'm sorry. It's just that I'm tired, so tired, and I want to spend what time I have left with you—not them." He jabs his thumb at Dr. Plaid.

The old guy smiles. "We're all half dead, Kid. It's a matter of extending one's life to make it as enjoyable as possible. Even if we can't cure you, we can make sure the end is as good as it can be."

Bryan's sharp gaze cuts to the man. "Don't patronize me. It's easy to say that when there's nothing wrong with you."

The old guy laughs and points a tongue depressor at Bryan. "And that's where you're wrong, Kid. We don't all go to group meetings or proudly wear our cancer card on our chests—though I think we should."

"You have cancer?" Bryan asks, shocked.

The old guy nods. "Yes sir, and it's gotten to the point that I don't see patients anymore, but I owed your aunt a favor, so here I am. The best cancer doctor around, and I'm dying of the same damned disease I've spent my life curing. Allow my colleague to take a look at you, then we'll compare and see if there's something we can do to make your life better—you can bet money on that." He squeezes Bryan's shoulder and leaves the room. The other male doctors follow, leaving us with Dr. Scribbles.

She's older than Dr. Goatee and a lot quieter when she finally speaks. "When you get headaches, where are they? Can you show me?" Bryan points, explaining as best he can. She nods. "Have they always been there?"

He's silent for a moment, thinking, and then shakes his head. "No, they moved. Originally it felt like a sinus headache that was behind my ears and eyes."

She nods as she takes in the information, writing, her eyes scanning her notes swiftly as she does so. She asks a few more questions, mostly about time—when did this happen, when did that happen— followed by an exam. She asks questions, poking and prodding, until Bryan is too exhausted to answer. He slumps back into his bed.

She sighs and stares at her papers, and

then looks up at Bryan before clutching the papers to her chest. "Let me talk to the others." She smiles at us and leaves.

When the door clicks shut, I look over at Bryan. I've been sitting in a chair across from him. "That was cryptic."

His arm is draped over his eyes. "Yeah, I thought she was going to bust out a measuring tape and suggest a coffin size."

"Bryan!"

"She took notes for two hours straight!"

I smile and laugh a little. "She was probably writing hate mail to your aunt. It's a hobby I plan on joining her in soon." Bryan laughs so hard he winces. I rush over and slip into the bed next to him. "I'm sorry, I didn't mean to make you hurt more."

He holds up a hand. I take it, and kiss the back. "Laughter is one of the only things keeping me sane." He smiles up at me and then lays down, placing his head in my lap.

"Me, too." We sit there for a long time, me gently stroking his hair while humming a lullaby I don't remember learning. I sing the notes softly, continuing even after he's asleep.

I never heard the door open, so I startle when I see Joselyn standing there.

She holds up her hands and then presses a finger to her lips. She studies her brother as if trying to see the cancer through his skin. Finally, she looks up at me and whispers, "Did they say anything?"

"Not yet," I whisper back.

"If they need me for anything, I'm here." She's so nervous. Her arms are wrapped around her middle and she's barely breathing. She thinks Bryan will die before he forgives her for splitting us up. Jos looks everywhere except at Bryan. Tucking a piece of hair behind her ear, she rushes on, "I'd give him a kidney if it would help. I mean it, Hallie. Make sure they know." She's wringing her hands, about to burst into tears again. Her navy blue top is made of flowing fabric. It's coupled with a pair of ripped jeans that cost a fortune. Jos looks straight into my eyes. "Anything he needs, ok. Be sure to tell him. I know he's mad at me and I wish I could undo everything. I'm so sorry, Hallie."

Bryan speaks, surprising both of us.

"I'm not mad at you, Jos. I'd love it if you were here when they came back. Sit. Stay." We both thought he was asleep.

Jos's lip quivers violently, but she manages to tame it and takes her seat. "I love you, Bry."

He smiles weakly. "Right back at you, Mini Twin."

Chapter 9

The silent doctor returns, the male doctors following behind. Bryan is lying down, but when he sees her, he slides up and rests his back against the headboard. Jos and I had been talking, remembering things from when we were all happy and healthy— before the break-up. If he wasn't dying I don't think I could have forgiven her, but I can't cause Jos a lifetime of grief for this one mistake. She thought she was looking out for her brother, and I can't say I wouldn't do the same to protect Maggie.

Dr. Scribbles clears her throat. Sean finds a place at the back of the room and leans his broad shoulders against a wall.

Constance stands front and center. "Well?" Her voice is strained, tight. She doesn't want to tell her sister that her son is truly dying.

Dr. Plaid and the other guys nod to Dr. Scribbles and her notepad. She looks around the room slowly from face to face, before clutching the notebook to her chest. "I know everyone is on edge waiting for an answer, so I'm not going to come to it slowly—he is dying. Every indication shows that the tumor is growing rapidly, causing the pain, dizziness, and vision disturbances. We know you were told that the location of his tumor makes it inoperable, but I disagree. It is operable."

As soon as she says the words, everyone reacts in their own way. Sean pushes off the wall, demanding more details. Constance demands to know why his previous doctors claimed it was inoperable. Bryan leans forward, like he's reaching for a dream that can't be real. I know that look and it scares me. There was something in the doctor's tone, something she didn't get to say because everyone started talking. I grip Bryan's hand and squeeze. We look at each other, too afraid to hope.

The female doctor tries to speak, but everyone is talking at once. Then there's a high pitched whistle. The doc with the goatee pulls his fingers out of his mouth, bows his head to his associate, and says, "Continue, Dr. Sten."

The woman is calm, but the Ferros unnerve her. I can see it in her eyes. She sucks in air and explains. "Listen, they were right and they were wrong. Performing the surgery to remove the entire tumor will kill him before the cancer gets the chance, but —and this is the part where I ask you to remain silent until I'm finished—there is a procedure that can be done to remove part of the tumor. By removing it in pieces, it would allow us to go in and take away the parts that aren't surrounding a crucial part of the brain. If that surgery goes well, we can try the final surgery and completely remove the growth. It's a prudent way to buy more time and make certain that we can remove the tumor. It's wrapped itself around parts of the brain that will cause extreme trauma if the surgery doesn't go well. Untreated, the tumor will kill him anyway. With surgery, he might live."

Bryan is the first to speak, "Might?"

"The odds are still very slim, Mr. Ferro."

Thoughtfully, Bryan asks, "Why wasn't this option suggested previously?"

"Your previous doctors did not make this suggestion because this option wasn't available to us before now." Dr. Scribbles looks at Constance, unsure if she should say anything else.

Constance rolls her eyes and swats a hand. "I had an acquaintance at the FDA expedite approval of a new project. It had been tabled due to the millions of dollars in old medical equipment it would render obsolete, were it available for use. I then gave a generous donation to our hospital to buy the machine. My acquaintance is taking care of the part where the government has been dragging its feet."

"What are the odds of success?" Jos asks, timidly. She looks so small, so afraid.

Dr. Sten looks over at her. "Not very good, I'm afraid. We don't have enough data yet and every surgery has risks. This one has more than others because of the location of the growth."

Sean asks, "Why break it into two

separate surgeries? Why not try to do it all at once? Especially if the risk is so high."

Dr. Goatee answers. "It's a precaution and buys us more time."

I'm missing something. Why do they need more time? I'm about to ask, but Bryan beats me to it. "You're not telling us something. I have a feeling Aunt Connie knows, but I need to be the one who decides, so tell me."

Dr. Sten places her clipboard down and walks toward us, stopping at the foot of the bed. "There's a chance your first doctor was right, that even with the new machine, we can't reach the growth. We're hoping that removing a piece of the mass will slow the cancer. Giving us more time, allows us to come up with more options, more treatments. However, if the cancer is more invasive than we'd thought—"

"Then you risked his life for nothing." Sean closes his eyes before pinching the bridge of his nose.

"It's not simple, Mr. Ferro. Nothing about this is easy." Dr. Sten looks over at Bryan. "You have so little time left."

"Yeah, but this could take it all away and

I don't want to waste any of it. That's what you're telling me, right? That if I do this, I may die anyway. And if you don't remove all of the tumor, it'll just come back. Do I understand you correctly, doctor?" His last words are angry, but he's trying to hide it.

Jon has been staring out the window. He turns and nods. "That's exactly what she's saying."

Dr. Sten's voice softens. "I can't tell you what to do. We only recommend surgery when the benefits outweigh the risks. In your case, the surgery is too new to know for certain. You may recover fully."

"Or he could die on the table." Sean is the master of bluntness.

Constance finally speaks up. "How long does he have?"

"A few weeks, maybe less. There's another problem." Dr. Sten looks over at the men.

Doc Plaid explains, "He's ripe for an aneurism. He can't move, been sitting or sleeping most of the day. Considering the rate at which that tumor is growing in his head, he could leave us at any time now."

The room is silent. No one speaks.

Prickles line my arms and neck. I want to yell at them and tell them they're wrong, so I bite my lip. The silence grows deafeningly loud until Bryan speaks. "So, I'm already dead. In which case, I should have the surgery. Is that your recommendation?"

They nod.

Bryan looks away and pulls his hand from mine. He pushes his hair out of his face and stands. I have no idea what he's doing or what he's going to say. "It's strange, you know. I don't feel like I'm dying, not right now. And the problem is, I'm not ready to leave yet. You're asking me to give up the little time I have left when the odds aren't in my favor anyway. If I was your kid, what would you do? If you had what I have, would you choose the surgery or live the last few minutes of your life the way you wanted?" He's standing in front of them, sincerely asking, but the doctors don't speak. Bryan works his jaw and his anger bursts free. "Answer me! I deserve that! There is no way in Hell you should ask me to do something that you wouldn't do yourself!" His fists are balled at his sides.

I don't expect anyone to answer, but

surprisingly, Dr. Sten speaks, her voice soothing, "I would do it, even with the risk. It's trading minutes for a lifetime. If things went well, you'll have a chance to start a family, to love the people you care about. If things go wrong on the operating table, well, you were dead anyway. To me, it's worth the risk. That's why I lingered. In your position I would choose surgery. My colleagues disagree, but I couldn't keep this option from you. I would choose it myself." She smiles kindly at him. "Knowing my answer won't help you make yours, Bryan. But it's the best we can offer you, and it's better than nothing."

Bryan stiffens as she speaks. Pain is flooding his body. I jump up and pull him back to the foot of the bed. "Sit. Here." I hand him more medicine. Bryan looks over at me with glassy eyes. He blinks once, hard, and a tear rolls down his cheek.

"I was supposed to watch out for you."

Keeping my voice as steady as possible, I hang my arm across his shoulders and pull him into my side. "You'll always be watching out for me, whether you're here or there."

My words choke him up more. He tries to pull away, but I won't let go. The cup of water is knocked out of my hand and his pills roll across the floor as he buries his face into my shoulder. "I'm not weak," he whispers.

"No one thinks you are," I whisper back. We stay like that for a few moments. Everyone is watching us, waiting for Bryan's answer. When he pulls away from my shoulder, he puts on his fake smile and stands.

Padding to Dr. Sten, he offers his hand. She takes it and shakes. "I don't understand."

"While all of you spoke truthfully, Dr. Sten, you told me how you felt and why. Will you be the doctor performing the surgery?"

She nods. "There will be several of us, including my colleagues present here today."

"But you will be the lead doctor, right?" She nods. "Then set it up."

Chapter 10

Two days. That's when they set the surgery that will most likely kill him. Everyone except Sean has gone. Bryan made his decision for better or worse, and doesn't want to talk about it. He's retreated behind fake smiles again and I can't blame him. He hides his fear so well. I wouldn't have thought he was afraid at all, but I know he is. The way he looks at me, the touch of his hand is almost panicked after he sits down next to me on his bed.

I don't want to leave him, but I have to go end things with Neil before he comes looking for me. "Stay with him until I get back?" I can't believe I'm asking Sean Ferro for a favor. He nods and remains in a dark corner like a snake waiting to strike. Sean freaks me out. Seriously. I'm glad he's on Bryan's side.

I grab my purse and look down at the oversized sweats. If this doesn't send a message, I don't know what will. "I'll be back in a little bit." I lean over to kiss Bryan on the forehead, but he pulls me down onto the bed and slows the kiss, licking the seam of my lips until I let him in. Butterflies swirl inside my stomach and I giggle, pushing him back when I remember we're being watched. "Bryan!"

"No more little kisses, not until I'm gone. Save that peck for the final kiss before they lower me into the ground."

His words stab me through the heart. I can barely breathe, but he looks up at me, holding onto my hands. "Hallie, the only time we have is right now. I've accepted it. The surgery isn't going to work. Promise me that you'll kiss me good-bye."

I try to smile, but my mouth doesn't want to move, so I nod. Bryan's dark lashes lower. "So, are you going to break things off with him or tell him that you'll be home in a few days?"

"You really think I could go back to him after all of this?" I stare in disbelief, my jaw hanging open. I glance back at Sean, but Bryan takes my cheek and turns me back toward him.

Looking into my eyes he says, "You should go back to him when this is done. You shouldn't be alone."

"How can you say that?"

"I won't be here anymore, Hallie. He was good to you."

"He told me to sleep with you so we could avoid a scandal. He wasn't good for me and I'm not staying with him. I'm sick of doing things the easy way. Besides, I won't be alone. I have Maggie. We'll watch out for each other, so don't worry about us." Bryan begins to protest, so I lean in and give him another lavish kiss. "I'll be back in an hour or so."

"All right. Then I have something fun planned."

"Do you?"

"Yes, so prepare yourself." He winks at me and I blush. "Damn, Hallie. I may need to send Sean away so I can have my way with you."

I smile and laugh. "In a little bit. I'll be right back." I glance up at Sean. He's emerged from his corner and pulls up a chair next to Bryan. For a second I have a horrible feeling in the pit of my stomach, like something is about to go horribly wrong.

"I've got this, Hallie. Go." Sean starts talking to Bryan about some new patent he's applying for and asks him how he chose his technology stocks. All business. Good. For a second, I was worried Sean was going to tell Bryan about Victor.

Chapter 11

"Neil?" I call his name as I shove through the front door of his condo. My plan is to end this nicely and walk away. I'll come after for the money when the time comes, but it's not right now. Touching the engagement ring on my finger, I twist, pulling it off. Neil should be parked in front of the computer playing WOW with his friends. That's his normal activity for right now and unplanned life will likely give way to chaos. He always says stuff like that, which is going to make this harder. He's going to think that I'm leaving him to be with Bryan, but that's not the whole of it. I don't want my life to be lived like this. It's not fair to me or him. Padding through the kitchen, I look around. Two cups are on the counter, empty. The coffee pot is still full and smells burnt. I walk over and turn it off.

An eerie feeling creeps up my spine as I look around. Something's off but I can't tell what. Everything is the way it usually is, so I shove my paranoia aside. "Neil?" I call his name again, but no answer.

I lean against the counter and turn back to look at the room. I can see straight through the house, all the way to the front door. Everything is meticulous, as it always is, but one thing is not. A chair—Neil's chair —at the kitchen table is pulled out and pivoted slightly. It looks like it was shoved in with one hand. My gaze rests on the chair. Even in a hurry, he wouldn't do something like that. I walk over and look at the piece of wood, wishing it could speak. I don't want to be here.

Gathering my courage, I hike up the stairs and stop in front of the closed door. "Neil, I know you're angry with me, but we need to talk. We can't go on like this. It's not good for either of us." I'm looking at the ring in my hand as I speak. Still no answer.

"Neil?"

Reaching up, I take the knob in my hand and twist. When the door swings open, I gag from the smell and stagger back, nearly falling down the staircase. My hand flies over my mouth and muffles my scream.

Neil.

Blood.

Cecily.

Their naked bodies are tangled together and lifeless. The pristine mattress and blankets are covered in old blood and the smell has me ready to vomit. I stand there for a moment, holding my stomach, bent over. My hair dangles in my face obscuring the person next to me. It's not until he speaks that I move.

"Did you forget about me? Because I have not forgotten about you." Victor is standing next to me with a hideous grin on his lips. He gazes at the dead couple on the bed. "I thought you'd never come back. Thank God for small miracles, because I owe you big time."

Sean's voice echoes through my mind. *He won't underestimate you again.*

I don't know what to do. I'm unarmed

and Victor has a gun in his belt and a knife in his hand. His silver blade is clean even though I'm sure that's why there's so much blood. "You killed them." I manage to choke out the words. My palms are on the wall, sliding along it, trying to not fall.

"It looks like some of my older work." He surveys the bed and grins. "It's personal, that's for fucking certain. The cops will wonder what kind of person did this, and they're going to assume it was you. You see, since your fiancée was banging this old lady, I killed an extra person. She wasn't part of the plan, but the woman saw me and right now everyone thinks I'm dead—thanks to you. I have to say that was a massive favor, sliding that blade across my neck. Everyone thought I was pushing up daisies somewhere, but you," he laughs and points his knife at my throat, "you didn't bury the blade in my neck, so here I am." He steps toward me. Before I can react, his knife comes into contact with my shoulder. I scream and pull away. The movement throws me off balance and before I can regain my footing, Victor pushes me. I go flying backwards down the staircase, slamming my head, shoulder, and face as I bounce down the steps.

I'm yelling at him, and trying to get to my feet, but he's faster than I am, and unharmed. The back of my head stings. I touch it and my fingers come away covered in blood.

"Get up." Victor kicks at me. "You're not some pampered ass little princess. Fight back."

"Leave. Go away right now and no one will ever know that you were here." I hold my shoulder, trying to stop the flow of blood as I stand. My head spins and the room tilts to the side. I'm going to die.

The man laughs. "And have you talk? Do I look dumb? The thing I can't believe is you saw firsthand what happens to a bitch that disappoints me. You have no idea what hell you're about to live through, do you? I'm going to make this long and slow."

"The neighbors will come. They'll hear me." I take a step back.

"The neighbors are ancient and can't hear jack shit without their hearing aids, which have gone missing. It's been a few days now, but I bet we have a few more to play around before anyone comes looking."

My body is covered in sweat and my mind is telling me to run, but my body wants to fight. The conflict is making it difficult to move, that and the blood pouring down my arm. "Where's Maggie?"

Victor grins showing off his gold tooth. "Where do you think? That bitch was good in bed, but loose lips aren't becoming. I took care of her. Too bad you weren't around to stop me this time." Without warning, he throws the knife in his hand. It flies by my ear and buries in the wall.

I shriek and whirl around, grabbing the first thing I see—Neil's chair. Victor is pulling his gun out, so he can't block my swing. I hurl the chair around in a fury and hear wood crack as it comes into contact with his body. Victor swears and the gun flies across the room and into the kitchen. As soon as the chair is out of my hands, I race for the door, but Victor grabs me.

We roll for a moment, and then he pins me to the floor. "You're not getting away this time, you fucking whore." His fist connects with my cheek and pain explodes behind my eye. I try to twist out of his grip, but I can't move. "You ready, slut? Things are going to get interesting."

Before I know what's happening, he pulls down my sweatpants. I'm not wearing panties because I didn't have extra clothes at Bryan's house. Victor continues, "I knew it. Fucking cunt. This part is fun. Have I told you that I prefer this area to be nice and smooth? How about a shave?"

I shake my head furiously, pleading incoherently.

"Fine, then we'll do it this way." He pulls out a lighter and flicks it. The thing flames to life. Victor keeps me pinned with one arm while his hand inches closer and closer to the hairy patch between my legs. As soon as the lighter touches the hair, the entire section catches fire. I scream and writhe, trying to get away from him, but I can't move. Tears flow down my cheeks as he watches my bush burn. He waits a moment, letting me shout out in pain, and then grabs me—crushing the fire with his hand.

"Let me go." I manage.

"Beg me not to fuck you senseless." His dark eyes lock on mine. "Do it." He moves his hand and a finger slips into me. He pushes hard and I scream.

We've shifted and I hadn't noticed. I take the shot, knowing it's the only one I'm going to get. My heel launches straight into his junk. Victor curls into a ball as I yank my pants up and run out of the house.

My heart is pounding so hard it feels like it's going to explode. I race past Bryan's car and don't look back. But I hear Victor behind me, getting closer and closer. I wanted to stay in a public area, but no one seems to be out. I run until I can't breathe. My lungs are on fire. I didn't think about where I was going, but I realize it when I see Bryan jump out of a car before it fully stops.

He rushes toward me. "Hallie!"

"No! Bryan, go!" I try to tell him, but I can barely speak. I crash into him, unable to breathe. He hands me off to Sean and walks toward my house. "No!" I scream and try to pull away.

Time stops. Victor steps into the middle of the street, gun pulled and aimed straight at me. He cocks it, and ignores Bryan until he can't.

"If you want her, you're going to have to

kill me first." Bryan's voice is level and strong. He's holding a gun, already cocked, straight at Victor's face.

"That cunt's not worth dying for."

"That's where you're wrong." Bryan fires and the shot rings out. There's an echo and at the last second Victor repositions his gun, but he falls to the ground.

Sean is holding onto my waist as I try to claw away from him. I'm screaming his name, watching the man I love fall to the earth in slow motion.

"It wasn't an echo!" I kick free from Sean and rush to Bryan.

Before I get there his body crumples to the ground. His eyes see me one last time before they roll back and stare at the sky. Blood flows from his chest, soaking his shirt and flowing onto the ground. "No, no, no! Make it stop! Sean! Help me!" I clutch Bryan's head and weep as life bleeds out of him.

"Love you. Always loved you." Bryan's voice is so weak, so filled with pain that it cuts me in half.

"I love you, too. Always have." I smile down at him and a peaceful look spreads across his face. Bryan becomes limp in my arms as I stroke his head and tell him that it will be okay.

Everything will be okay.

Chapter 12

Police lights flash around us, and I don't understand what they're saying. Someone is pulling me away while another cop takes Bryan's gun. "Run the numbers on that."

"Yes sir." He takes the weapon and disappears.

Sean is standing over us, stiff and silent.

A cop asks if we were engaged. He found a ring on the ground. I don't answer. I can't answer. My voice has been sucked away and there are no words.

The voices around me are a blur of noise until Sean speaks. "No, it was mine."

"Mr. Ferro, this weapon was used in another homicide."

I glance over because Sean sits down hard. He says a name—a woman's name—like it's a blessing and a curse. He breathes in deeply and rubs his eyes before looking at his cousin with a strange smile on his face. "You fucking idiot."

I don't understand. "What are you talking about?" Sean won't answer, he just shakes his head. His eyes are hard and unfeeling. I want to scream at him, but I can't.

A cop answers me. "This is the gun that killed Amanda Ferro."

Chapter 13

Consumed by shock and emotional overload, I can't process what he's telling me. I blink at him. "What?"

"They couldn't find the weapon during the trial, but everyone thought Sean Ferro killed her." Sean has walked away, his shoulders stiffen with each word and I know he can hear. Grief is tearing through me, but something feels wrong.

"I don't understand." I wipe the tears off my face and smear them across my cheek. "What are you saying?"

"I'm saying what it looks like, Miss Raymond. Although we can't be entirely conclusive at this point, it points the blame for that murder in another direction. It looks like Bryan Ferro shot Amanda, and for whatever reason Sean willingly took the blame." The cop is old enough to remember the trial. He stares after Sean with respect in his eyes. It's not the typical animosity that people offer when they see the man. They think he's a heartless monster and Sean's become that person. In Bryan's bedroom I'd seen old pictures of the boys when they were young. Sean smiled then and his eyes didn't have that hollow, creepy thing they have now. It's like he's been carrying around a massive secret and I can't bear to think that this cop is telling me the truth. Bryan is dead because of me. He walked straight into the line of fire to protect me, so why the hell would he kill Sean's wife? I straighten and turn to look at Sean.

He's rigid and trembling, trying to walk away, but he keeps looking over his shoulder until he stops and turns. Arms folded over that strong chest, he stares at his cousin's lifeless body with a look that walks the line between disdain and admiration.

I can't stand it. Something inside of me breaks. In a rage of tears and fury, I jump up and race toward him, screaming wildly. When I collide into his chest, he barely moves but it doesn't stop me from throwing punches. I connect my fist with his rock hard side once, before he grabs my wrist. Yanking me close, he hisses in my face, "You're not the only one grieving right now."

I pull my arm away and nearly stumble backward. The cops watch us, but no one intercedes since Sean seems calm. He may be steady, but I'm not. I knew Bryan wouldn't be with me much longer but Sean stole the few extra minutes we had, and then this—the humiliation. In his death, Bryan will be slandered and accused of a murder there's no way he committed. I hiss up at Sean, "It's a lie. He didn't kill her."

"How would you know?" Sean's voice is cold and detached, although his gaze lingers on Bryan as they shift his body to a black bag.

I glance over at him and fall to my knees sobbing. "He wouldn't have been here tonight if you didn't make me break things off with Neil! This is your fault! You told him! He wouldn't have come if you didn't tell him about Victor!" I pound the pavement with my hands until they're raw and bleeding. Sean doesn't answer, which makes me furious. "Admit it!" I'm in his face again, speaking in a death whisper. "Bryan wouldn't have died tonight if it wasn't for you."

Two words. That's all he says. "You're right."

I start sobbing again and let out a scream. By now there's a police line and paramedics. The EMTs try to look at me, but I can't leave Bryan. When they zip the bag shut, I beg them to stop. "He'll be all right." I claw the guy's arm as he zips the bag. "Please stop! I can't do this again! I can't! He'll be all right! He has to be!"

Sean pulls me away and smashes me to his chest. His eyes are glassy, but there's not a single tear shed. I hate him. I rip away from his grip and spit on his face. Sean doesn't move to wipe it off. People watching us are holding out cameras. That's when I feel a hand on my shoulder.

I turn around, expecting it to be a cop, but it's not. A wall of red hair greets me with a sad smile. "I told you I'd be there for you. Why didn't you call me?"

Chapter 14

Maggie takes hold and hugs me hard, letting me fall apart in her embrace. She whispers nonsense and strokes the hair off my face.

She helps the paramedics get me into an ambulance to look me over. When I sit down, I wince. The guy is young, but he realizes what it means. He calls for a female worker and a cop comes over. She's a tiny thing, and her gaze is sympathetic. "Honey, I need to talk to you." She climbs into the bus and closes one of the doors so that no one else can hear. "Did Victor Campone rape you?"

I don't know what to say. Shaking my

head, I tell her what happened. It feels so long ago even though the burns on my skin are fresh. I haven't felt them until now. "My skin burns."

"Let me get someone to check you, then. We need to see how the burns are so we can treat them. Okay, honey? You've been through enough tonight. Let them help you." The cop is watching me with pity in her eyes. She sees the ring on my hand. I put it back there without thinking. They assumed I was engaged to Bryan. They don't know about Neil and Cecily yet, so I tell them. Her eyes go wide and she talks quickly into her shoulder. I add, "I think he went into the surrounding homes as well. Please check on them. Mr. Thom was always nice to me." I start balling again when I realize that Victor may have killed him too.

A medic is by me, but I can't calm down. "Who's your next of kin?" The medic keeps asking, which makes me cry more. No one. I'm alone.

Maggie says soothing words and tries to calm me down. I hold her hand like a frightened child and look up at her. She smiles up at me. "I'm not going anywhere. We're in this together. I told you."

"Maggie is my next of kin." I point at her and sign something. They start to ask her how to treat me since I'm not coherent. I ramble and cry when I should say something. The police try to ask me questions, but the more they ask the faster I fall apart. It's Sean who puts a stop to it.

His loud voice booms from the other side of the door. "I saw the shooting. Ask me. Miss Raymond has been through enough for tonight."

"We need more information."

Sean's voice drops. He says something I can't make out, but it ends with, "Her lawyer is here and if you want to play nice, I suggest you show some compassion right now. She won't forget this night. None of the details will fade from her mind. Leave her alone for now."

Maggie is watching me on the gurney. I'm laying down because sitting hurts. I wonder how much skin I have left and what this will do to me. I'll be scarred forever in one of the most intimate places on my body, but I can't manage to care. I keep thinking about Bryan in that cold bag. The hysterical sobbing starts again and Maggie asks them to give me something.

A needle is shoved into my arm. Maggie sings softly, as she strokes my forehead. Suddenly my eyelids feel like lead. They flutter as I try to keep them open. Sean appears between blinks and asks about me. With Maggie's consent, they tell him what Victor did to me. He doesn't say a word. The man just stares at me like I'm a piece of trash, like his cousin's life wasn't worth this.

"He loved me." The words sound strong and proud in my mind, but they fall over my lips as a whisper.

"Without a doubt." Sean replies and stands there, watching me fall asleep.

Epilogue

The wind cuts through my coat as I walk to the grave, my bundle close to my chest. I shouldn't be here, but I had to come. I'm drawn here every few months. I have to talk to him and this seems like the place to do it. Bryan promised he'd always be with me, and although I know he is, it's still hard. The baby is asleep in my arms, indifferent to the chill in the air. I have him bundled from head to toe and hold onto him tight.

Since the night Bryan died, so many things have happened. I felt so alone without him, or so I thought until a few weeks after Bryan's death. A pregnancy test affirmed my suspicion and I carried a baby boy to term. He has bright green eyes, just like his daddy. He's my life now. Maggie, the baby and I live together, an unlikely but content family. I still write—a bleeding heart never heals and the pages call to me. Writing gives me peace when things get unbearable.

I stop in front of my father's grave first and tell him about his grandson. "I gave him my name, Dad. Well, your name. I don't want them to know about him. If they find out…" That's my biggest fear. What if the Ferros find out about little Bryan Raymond? What if they find out he's the only son of Bryan, the youngest heir to that fucking fortune? They'll take him from me. I know they will. So I gave him my name and when the papers asked, I said he was Neil's. That we were getting married. The papers ran wild with articles about Neil and me, depicting us as a modern day Romeo and Juliet. They couldn't have been further from the truth. Meanwhile, Bryan was linked to the murder of Amanda Ferro and another man they found in the woods. The gun had been used several times. Bryan wasn't a murderer. The only person he ever killed was Victor, and he did it to save me. I don't care what forensics say. Eventually, I stopped reading articles about him. During his trail, the way they'd written about Sean was horrible, but the way they slandered Bryan was far worse. I avoid newspapers and stay off of Huffington Post. I live in a bubble with Maggie and my baby.

After talking to Daddy, I risk it. The cemetery isn't exactly bursting with visitors today. It's too cold. I walk over to Bryan's tomb, a huge mausoleum with FERRO marked on the outside. Originally, the family wasn't going to allow him to be buried with them, but Sean fought them on it, so here he is—my lost love. I lean against the heavy door, pushing it mostly closed. I don't want anyone to know I was here, so I keep it dark inside, lit only by what sunshine can make its way through the door. It's overcast today, so it's darker than usual. I shift baby Bryan in my arms as he wakes up. He smiles up at me with the same grin his daddy wore so many times before.

"We're visiting Daddy," I tell him and loosen his blankets. "He was a great man and he loves you very much. Right now,

Daddy can see us. He'll watch over you, Bryan." I'm standing in front of Bryan's tomb with my back to the door. I never heard him enter.

When he speaks, his voice is softer than his brothers' voices. "Hallie?"

I startle and whirl around. Peter Ferro is standing in the door surrounded by light. He looks like an angel as he steps into the large room. He's wearing a tweed coat and slacks. He's a principal somewhere in Jersey. I've seen him around, but we never talked much. I hadn't thought he was close to Bryan, but I must have guessed wrong, otherwise he wouldn't be here.

"I'm sorry. I'm leaving." I go to walk past him, but Peter won't let me. He steps in front of me and smiles.

"You don't have to go. I'll never run you off, and I'll never tell them—but they're going to notice."

I play dumb because I have no other option. Fear is choking me and I can barely spit out the words. "Notice what? That I came in here to say goodbye to someone I loved? They already know that. And Constance never contested Bryan's will, so I think I'm good."

"You know what I mean." He looks down at the baby.

Bryan gazes up at Peter with his daddy's big green eyes and dark glossy hair. "I'm afraid not." I bundle the baby, and step around Peter, about to step outside when he stops me in my tracks.

"That's Bryan's baby. They could force a paternity test to prove it, Hallie. If my mother doesn't already know, she soon will. She won't let a Ferro grow up outside of the mansion."

I don't deny it. "You grew up there. Tell me, would you want your child to live that life?"

"I can't change the past, Hallie, and neither can you."

"I know that. You don't think I know that this is my fault that his daddy is here because of me? I blamed Sean and Constance. I even blamed Jon, but the only reason Bryan showed up that night was because of me. And then everything that followed." I can't even say it.

Peter says with utter certainty. "The media was wrong. Look at what they did with you and Neil. Are you telling me all the shit was true?"

I laugh bitterly. "Far from it."

"So, don't let them ruin your memories of him. Bryan didn't kill Amanda." He sounds so certain.

"How can you know that?"

"Because I was with him that night and it makes no sense. He liked Amanda. We all did."

Something from the night of Bryan's murder comes back to mind—a memory of Sean standing there looking horrified. "He didn't know Bryan had that gun, did he?"

Peter laughs once, softly, and shakes his head. "Sean never talks about Amanda or that night, but I agree with you on that point."

I glance up at Peter. "While Bryan was dying, Sean called him a fucking idiot. He was so mad. I thought it was because he got shot."

"I think it was because Bryan wasn't supposed to have that weapon. Hallie, he saved you and his baby, but he also saved a few other people in the process. He gave Sean his life back. Bryan was selfless. He'd do anything he could to help someone. If taking that gun helped, if taking the blame helped, he'd have done it in a heartbeat. Don't you think?"

I nod. There's silence as we both stare at Bryan's final resting place. "That's why Sean fought for him to be here. Bryan didn't kill those people."

"I suspect that's the case."

"As does Sean."

Peter gives a crooked smile. "Most likely." After a moment, he adds, "You shouldn't come here anymore, not if you want that child to grow up apart from the rest of the family. Actually, it would be good if you, Bryan, and Maggie picked up and moved. Go somewhere they won't find you, not for a while, at least. Make it hard for them to see the baby or get pictures of him. It'll buy you time—time you won't have if you stay here." He brushes his finger against the baby's cheek. "He looks just like his daddy."

"I know." I beam at my little bundle as he coos at Peter.

"Here." He hands me his card. "If you ever need anything, just ask. I never saw you and I never saw Bryan's baby." He winks at me then slips through the door, his hands in his pockets and his head hung between his shoulders.

I call after him. "Peter, wait." I hurry out into the crisp air. "Am I doing the right thing? He has family. It's the one thing I never had and always wanted. I've wondered if keeping him from them is the right thing to do."

"He has family, Hallie. He has you and Maggie. He's not missing a thing. I hear parts of Montana are beautiful. Go check it out." Peter smiles at us and walks away.

After Bryan died I never thought I'd love again. I felt my heart fracture and a piece of me died along with him. Blackness consumed me until that little plastic stick read PREGNANT. Bryan's baby was strong and healed my broken heart as he grew inside of me. Now that he's here, in my arms, I see his daddy's face every day and know I'm blessed.

After getting Bryan into his car seat, I get in and close the door. After starting the engine, I press a button and call Maggie. "Hey, how do you feel about Montana?"

"Can I have a horse?"

"What do you want a horse for, you don't know how to ride one?" I smile and look over at Bryan's grave, knowing I'll never see it again. Maggie is babbling about horses and I finally cut her off, "Yes, you can have a horse."

"I'm in. When do we leave?"

"Tonight. They can't find him, Maggie, and one of the Ferros already knows the truth. Are you sure you want to come? You don't have to." This isn't a little thing to ask, and I know it. I don't want to be selfish and take her with me into the middle of nowhere.

"Fuck, yeah. There's like miles of nothing. I'm going to dress in chaps and wear a huge ass hat, and buy a pony. Yes, I'm coming!" She laughs. "You're such a dork, you know that? I'm your sister— maybe not by birth, but by choice. That's the best kind, you know. I'll call and set up the jet. We'll be out of here in a few hours, Hallie. It'll be good for you and little cutie baby Bryan. We can live on a ranch!"

I laugh, surprised at how easy it was to talk her into it. Then it dawns on me. "You knew we'd have to leave, didn't you?"

"Someday, yeah, especially if you wanted to hide Bryan from the Ferros. But I thought you were going to pick some place lame like a swamp. I'm all over Montana. I hear they have sexy cowboys. I've never ridden a cowboy."

"Maggie!"

She laughs. "Come home. I'll get our stuff together. You're ready for this Hallie. It's a good move. See you in a bit." She hangs up.

I tip my head back against the seat as I gaze at Bryan's tomb, and listen to his son make happy sounds in the back seat wondering if I'm making the right decision.

"I wish you were here. I wish you could tell me what to do." I say the words into the air, talking to my lost love.

I'm not big into wishing for anything. As an orphan, I learned it's a waste of time, but right as I say those words a ray of light cuts through the gray sky. A single shaft of sun shines down and touches the top of the Ferro's mausoleum. The copper dome gleams and my entire body covers in tingles. The wind softens and I swear Bryan's here, telling me to go.

I close my eyes, say a prayer, and when I look up the golden light is gone. For the first time since his death, peace flows through me and I welcome it. Putting the car into drive, I speak over my shoulder to my little man, "Bryan, we're going someplace fun, and I'm pretty sure Aunt Maggie is getting you a pony.

NEW RELEASES

To ensure you don't miss H.M. Ward's next book, text AWESOMEBOOKS (one word) to 22828 and you will get an email reminder on release day.

*****

Want to talk to other fans?
Go to Facebook and join the discussion!

COMING SOON

BROKEN PROMISES
A Trystan Scott Novel

MORE FERRO FAMILY BOOKS

NICK FERRO
~THE WEDDING CONTRACT~
*****

BRYAN FERRO
~THE PROPOSITION~
*****

SEAN FERRO
~THE ARRANGEMENT~
******

PETER FERRO GRANZ
~DAMAGED~
******

JONATHAN FERRO
~STRIPPED~
******

TRYSTAN SCOTT
~COLLIDE~
******

MORE ROMANCE BOOKS BY H.M. WARD

DAMAGED

DAMAGED 2

STRIPPED

SCANDALOUS

SCANDALOUS 2

SECRETS

THE SECRET LIFE OF TRYSTAN SCOTT

And more.

To see a full book list, please visit:
www.SexyAwesomeBooks.com/books.htm

CAN'T WAIT FOR H.M. WARD'S NEXT STEAMY BOOK?

★★★★★

Let her know by leaving stars and telling her
what you liked about
The Proposition 5
in a review!